Eleanor Coerr

SADAKO

ILLUSTRATED BY

Ed Young

G.P. Putnam's Sons · New York

With thanks to George Levenson,
for his vision, persuasion,
and undivided attention
throughout the project.

Text copyright © 1993 by Eleanor Coerr
Illustrations copyright © 1993 by Ed Young
This book was inspired by *Sadako and*
the Thousand Paper Cranes, a half-hour video.

G. P. Putnam's Sons, a division of The Putnam & Grosset
Group, 200 Madison Avenue, New York, NY 10016.
Published simultaneously in Canada.
Printed in Hong Kong by South China Printing Co. (1988) Ltd.
G. P. Putnam's Sons is a trademark of The Putnam
Berkley Group, Inc. Registered in the
U.S. Patent and Trademark Office.
Text set in Berkeley Old Style Medium
Lettering by David Gatti
Library of Congress Cataloging-in-Publication Data
Coerr, Eleanor. Sadako: by Eleanor Coerr; illustrated
by Ed Young. p   cm. Summary: Hospitalized
with the dreaded atom bomb disease, leukemia,
a child in Hiroshima races against time to fold
one thousand paper cranes to verify the legend that
by doing so a sick person will become healthy.
1. Leukemia in children—Juvenile literature.   2. Sasaki, Sadako,
1943–1955—Juvenile literature.   3. Atomic bomb—
Physiological effect—Juvenile literature.   4. Hiroshima-shi
(Japan)—History—Bombardment, 1945. [1. Leukemia.
2. Sasaki, Sadako, 1943–1955.   3. Atomic bomb—Physiological
effect.   4. Hiroshima-shi (Japan)—History—Bombardment, 1945.
5. Death.]   I. Young, Ed. ill.   II. Title.   RJ416.L4C63   1993
362.1′9699419′0092—dc20   [B]   92-41483   CIP   AC
ISBN 0-399-21771-1
7   9   10   8

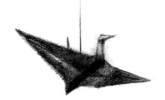

To the children of Hiroshima

One morning in August 1954, Sadako Sasaki looked up at the blue
sky over Hiroshima and saw not a cloud in the sky. It was a good sign.
Sadako was always looking for good-luck signs.

Back in the house, her sister and brothers were still sleeping on their bed quilts. She poked her big brother, Masahiro.

"Get up, lazybones!" she said. "It's Peace Day!"

Masahiro groaned, but when he sniffed the good smell of bean soup, he got up. Soon Mitsue and Eiji were awake, too.

Rushing like a whirlwind into the kitchen, Sadako cried, "Mother, can we please hurry with breakfast? I can hardly wait for the carnival!"

"You must not call it a carnival," her mother said. "It is a memorial day for those who died when the atom bomb was dropped on our city. Your own grandmother was killed, and you must show respect."

"But I do respect Obasan," Sadako said. "It's just that I feel so happy today."

At breakfast, Sadako fidgeted and wriggled her bare toes. Her thoughts were dancing around the Peace Day of last year—the crowds, the music, and the fireworks. She could almost taste the spun cotton candy.

She jumped up when there was a knock at the door. It was Chizuko, her best friend. The two were as close as two pine needles on the same twig.

"Mother, may we go ahead to the Peace Park?" Sadako asked.

"Yes, Sadako chan," her mother answered. "Go slowly in this heat!" But the two girls were already racing up the dusty street.

Mr. Sasaki laughed. "Did you ever see Sadako walk when she could run, hop, or jump?"

At the entrance to the Peace Park, people filed through the memorial building in silence. On the walls were photographs of the ruined city after the atom bomb—the Thunderbolt—had instantly turned Hiroshima into a desert.

"I remember the Thunderbolt," Sadako whispered. "There was the flash of a million suns. Then the heat prickled my eyes like needles."

"How could you possibly remember anything?" Chizuko exclaimed. "You were only a baby then."

"Well, I do!" Sadako said stubbornly.

After a speech by the mayor, hundreds of white doves were freed from their cages. Then, when the sun went down, a dazzling display of fireworks lit up the dark sky.

Afterward, everyone carried rice-paper lanterns to the banks of the Ohta River. Written on the rice paper were the names of relatives and friends who had died because of the Thunderbolt. Sadako had written Obasan's name on hers.

Candles were lit inside the lanterns. Then they were launched on the river, floating out to sea like a swarm of fireflies.

It was the beginning of autumn when Sadako rushed into the house with the good news.

"The most wonderful thing has happened!" she said breathlessly. "The big race on Field Day! I've been chosen to be on the relay team!" She danced around the room. "If we win, I'll be sure to get on the team next year!"

That was what Sadako wanted more than anything else.

From then on, Sadako thought of only one thing—the relay race. She practiced every day at school and often ran all the way home. Masahiro timed her with their father's big watch.

Sadako dreamed of running faster. Maybe, she thought, I will be the best runner in the whole world.

At last the big day arrived. Parents, relatives, and friends gathered at the school to watch the sports events. Sadako was so nervous she was afraid her legs wouldn't work at all.

"Don't worry," Mrs. Sasaki said. "When you get out there, you will run as fast as you can."

At the signal to start, Sadako forgot everything but the race. When it was her turn, she ran with all the strength she had. Her heart thumped painfully against her ribs when the race was over.

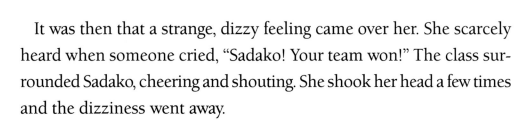

It was then that a strange, dizzy feeling came over her. She scarcely heard when someone cried, "Sadako! Your team won!" The class surrounded Sadako, cheering and shouting. She shook her head a few times and the dizziness went away.

All winter long, Sadako practiced to improve her speed. But every now and then the dizziness returned. She didn't tell anyone about it, not even Chizuko. Frightened, Sadako kept the secret inside of her.

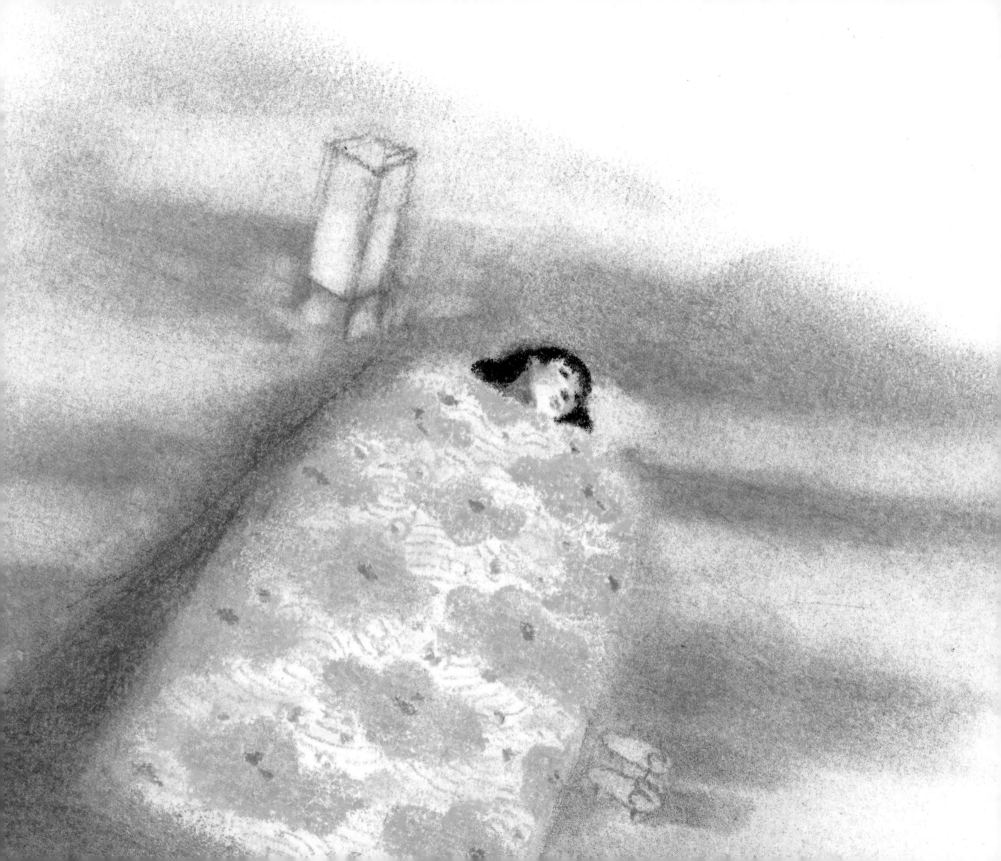

On New Year's Eve, Mrs. Sasaki hung good-luck symbols above the door to protect her family all through the year.

"As soon as we can afford it, I'll buy a kimono for you," she promised Sadako. "A girl your age should have one."

Sadako politely thanked her mother, but she didn't care about a kimono. She only cared about racing with the team next year.

For several weeks it seemed that the good-luck symbols were working. Sadako felt strong and healthy, and she ran faster and faster.

But all that ended one crisp, cold winter day in February when Sadako was running in the school yard. Suddenly everything seemed to whirl around her, and she sank to the ground.

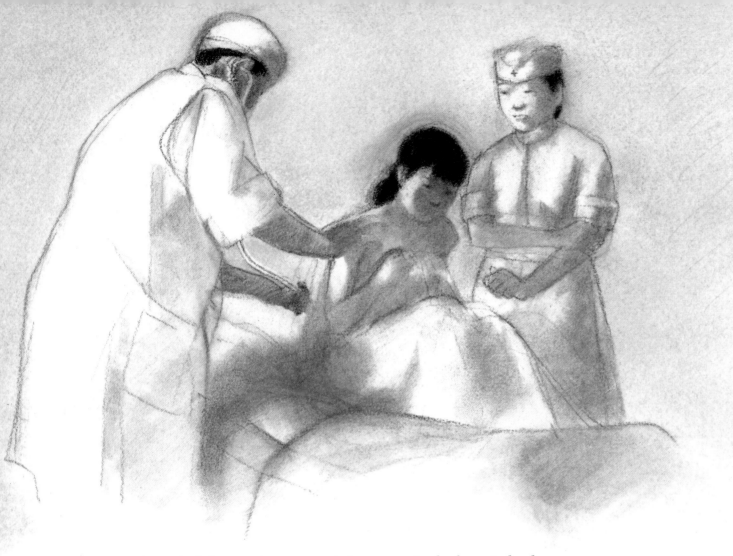

Soon Sadako was in an examining room in the hospital, where a nurse took some of her blood. Dr. Numata tapped her back and asked a lot of questions.

Sadako heard the doctor say the word "leukemia." That was the sickness caused by the atom bomb! She put her hands over her ears, not wanting to hear any more.

Mrs. Sasaki put her arms around Sadako. "You must stay here for a little while," she said. "But I'll come every evening."

"Do I really have the atom-bomb disease?" Sadako asked anxiously.

"The doctors want to take some tests, that's all," her father told her. "They might keep you here a few weeks."

A few weeks! To Sadako it seemed like years. What about the relay team?

When her family had left for the night, Sadako buried her face in the pillow and cried for a long time. She had never felt so lonely.

The next day, Chizuko came to visit, smiling mysteriously.

"Close your eyes," she said. Sadako held her eyes tightly shut. "Now you can look!"

Sadako stared at the paper and scissors on the bed. "What's that for?"

"I've figured out a way for you to get well," Chizuko said proudly. "Watch!"

She cut a piece of gold paper into a large square and folded it over and over, until it became a beautiful crane.

Sadako was puzzled. "But how can that paper bird make me well?"

"Don't you remember that old story about the crane?" Chizuko asked. "It's supposed to live for a thousand years. If a sick person folds one thousand paper cranes, the gods will grant her wish and make her well again."

She handed the golden crane to Sadako. "Here's your first one."

"Thank you, Chizuko chan," Sadako whispered. "I'll never part with it."

That night, Sadako felt safe and lucky. She set to work folding cranes, and Masahiro hung them from the ceiling. Why, in a few weeks she would be able to finish the thousand cranes and go home—all well again.

Eleven...I wish I'd get better...

Twelve...I wish I'd get better...

One day Nurse Yasunaga wheeled Sadako out onto the porch for some sunshine. There Sadako met Kenji. He was nine and small for his age, with a thin face and shining dark eyes.

Soon the two were talking like old friends. Kenji had been in the hospital a long time, but his parents were dead and he had few visitors.

"It doesn't really matter," Kenji said with a sigh, "because I'll die soon. I have leukemia from the bomb."

Sadako didn't know what to say. She wanted so much to comfort him. Then she remembered. "You can make paper cranes like I do," she said, "so that a miracle can happen!"

"I know about the cranes," Kenji said quietly. "But it's too late. Even the gods can't help me now."

That night, Sadako folded a big crane out of her prettiest paper and
sent it across the hall to Kenji's room. Perhaps it would bring him luck.
Then she made more birds for her own flock.
One hundred ninety-eight…I wish I'd get better…
One hundred ninety-nine…I wish I'd get better…

One day Kenji didn't appear on the porch, and Sadako knew that Kenji had died.

Late that night, Sadako sat at the window, letting the tears come. After a while, she felt the nurse's gentle hand on her shoulder.

"Do you think Kenji is out there on a star island?" Sadako asked.

"Wherever he is, I'm sure he is happy now," the nurse replied. "He has shed that tired, sick body, and his spirit is free."

"I'm going to die next, aren't I?"

"Of course not!" Nurse Yasunaga answered with a firm shake of her head. "Come, let me see you fold another crane before you go to sleep. After you finish one thousand, you'll live to be an old, old lady."

Sadako tried hard to believe that. She folded birds and made the same wish. Now there were more than three hundred cranes.

In July it was warm and sunny, and Sadako seemed
to be getting better.

"I'm over halfway to a thousand cranes," she told
Masahiro, "so something good is going to happen."

And it did.

Her appetite came back and much of the pain went away. She was going to get to go home for O Bon, the biggest holiday of the year. O Bon was a special celebration for spirits of the dead who returned to visit their loved ones on earth.

Mrs. Sasaki and Mitsue had scrubbed and swept the house, and the air was filled with smells of delicious holiday food. Dishes of bean cakes and rice balls had been placed on the altar.

After they had eaten, Eiji handed Sadako a big box
tied with a red ribbon. Slowly Sadako opened it. Inside
was a silk kimono with cherry blossoms on it. Sadako
felt hot tears blur her eyes.

"Why did you do it?" she asked, stroking the soft
cloth. "Silk costs so much money."

"Sadako chan," her father said gently, "your mother stayed up late last night to finish sewing it. Try it on for her."

Mrs. Sasaki helped her put on the kimono and tie the sash. Everyone agreed that she looked like a princess.

Sadako let out a happy sigh. Perhaps—just perhaps— she was home to stay.

But by the end of the week Sadako was weak again and had to return to the hospital. The class sent her a Kokeshi doll to cheer her up. Sadako placed it on the bedside table next to the golden crane.

For the next few days, Sadako drifted in and out of a strange kind of half-sleep. Her parents sat beside the bed.

"When I die," she said dreamily, "will you put my favorite bean cakes on the altar for my spirit? And put a lantern on the Ohta River for me on Peace Day?"

Mrs. Sasaki could not speak. She took her daughter's hand and held it tightly.

"Hush!" Mr. Sasaki said. "That will not happen for many, many more years. Don't give up now, Sadako chan. You have to make only a few hundred more cranes."

As Sadako grew weaker, she wondered, Did it hurt to die? Or was it like falling asleep? Would she live on a heavenly mountain or star?

She fumbled with a piece of paper and clumsily folded one more bird.

Six hundred forty-four…

Her mother came in and felt her forehead. She gently took the paper away. As Sadako closed her eyes, she heard her mother whisper,

"O flock of heavenly cranes,
  Cover my child with your wings."

When she opened her eyes again, Sadako saw her family there beside the bed. She looked around at their faces and smiled. She knew that she would always be a part of that warm, loving circle.

Sadako looked up at the flock of paper cranes hanging from the ceiling. As she watched, a light autumn breeze made the birds rustle and sway. They seemed to be alive, and flying out through the open window.

Sadako sighed and closed her eyes. How beautiful and free they were.

Sadako Sasaki died on October 25, 1955.

Her friends and classmates worked together to fold 356 paper cranes, so that she would be buried with one thousand. In a way, she got her wish. She will live on in the hearts of all the people who hear her story.

The class collected Sadako's letters and writings and published them in a book called *Kokeshi*, after the doll they had given her. A Folded Crane Club was organized in her honor.

Sadako's friends began to dream of a monument to her and all the children who were killed by the bomb. Young people throughout the country helped collect money. They wrote letters and shared Sadako's story. Finally, in 1958, their dream came true.

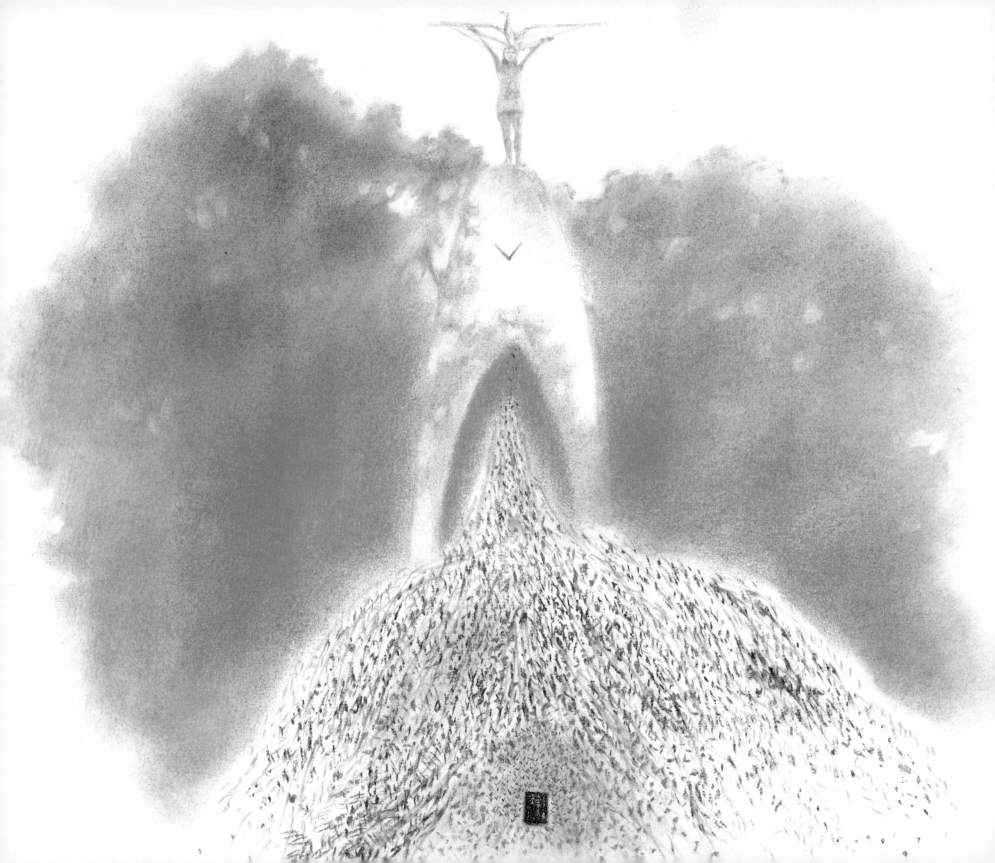

Now there is a statue of Sadako in Hiroshima Peace Park. She is standing on the Mountain of Paradise, holding a golden crane in outstretched hands.

Every year, on Peace Day, children hang garlands of paper cranes under the statue. Their wish is engraved at its base:

This is our cry,
this is our prayer:
Peace in the world.